Under Contract

Also by ASHLEY MURPHY

Daddy's Briefcase

Under Contract

Life in the Middle of Dreams

Ashley Murphy

Under Contract

Ashley Murphy
ashleysartcloset.blogspot.com
ashleysartcloset@yahoo.com

First Edition
Published in the United States

ISBN-13: 978-0-9831413-0-3
ISBN-10: 0-9831413-0-4

Library of Congress Control Number:
2016908906

Editor: Katelyn Murphy
Cover Design: Ashley Murphy

For you, reader…

In silence, reach for hidden
dreams within your soul. For
every dream reaches a goal.

God wants to use you for what
only you are able to reach.

Let your light shine.

Dream!

Life in the Middle of Dreams

In a firm downward motion, I
nudged my laptop closed.

My feet wiggled in front of me
touching the floor. The muscles
stiffened in my bent legs pushed
me to a stance.

"Hey girls, do you want to ride to
the grocery store with me?"

Both Gracie and Elizabeth parade toward the back entrance of our home.

Our family car parked on the other side of the door.

Upward, my fingertips reach touching the garage opener, mounted on the doorframe.

The passenger side front and the back door opened simultaneously.

Both girls climbed in, one in the front, one in the back.

Their faces held smiles.

Around the lift gate side of the car, my feet shuffled. After I open the driver side door, my bottom end pushed against the seat.

Then my ivory palm slipped on the car door handle pulling it towards me.

The brake pedal pushed down by my right foot. After, the gearshift rest in my hand, I slip the car in reverse.

The car wheels roll backwards. Brake. Drive. Then the wheels roll forwards a great distance on our driveway.

Glimpses of white, through heavy
sweet bay tree brush, caught our
eyes.

Elizabeth sat in the lite tan rider
seat next to me. She spoke up,
"Oh, it's the mailman. Mom. Stop."

The wheels barely touching our
street, I press the brake.

Stopped.

Elizabeth opens her door. Then
she strolled over to the jet-black
mailbox.

She lifted her right hand in the air
waving as the
mailperson continued on his
route.

A pile of mail covered her arm.

Gracie's head pressed forward
staring at her handheld game
device.

In the fall, Gracie will enter 3rd grade. The girl prefers to hunt with her dad. Her recreational sport of preference is soccer.

She loves playing on those green, grassy fields. Her favorite color is blue.

No matter what, she beams on and off the soccer field. Most games she holds her own in the goal.

Often, I mention she will be the next goal kicker for the high school football team.

She always laughs.

For now, nevertheless, I realize my daughter will continue dirt bike riding.

Elizabeth will start 11th grade in the fall.

She prefers to watch movies and talk on the phone with classmates.

Her favorite color is pink.

Mad organizing skills help her maintain the volleyball manager title at the academy she attends.

Each season, I look in her brown eyes speaking encouraging words, "You should play Elizabeth."

She responds, "Mom!"

Her soul shines brighter than a shooting star.

6

The car abruptly crossed double yellow lines in the middle of the street.

My head yanked forward. Then my blue eyes grew big confirming no cars approaching on the other side of the hill.

On to my heart dropping in the pit of my stomach saying, "Thank You, Jesus."

People call me "MG", short for Marcy Gene. Mom says she named me after my grandmother.

Both hands gripped the stirring wheel, jerking the tires back over the double lines.

Out of the corner of my eyes, I spotted glances of my girls. Their eyes emerge wide open. Their backs sat straight up in their seats.

The car ride continued to the local grocery.

My mouth remained shut. My eyesight glued to the road.

Elizabeth's left pointer finger stuck out against the translucent window. She tapped toward an empty parking place.

A few steps from the front door, I pulled my car between two white lines. Finally, we entered the grocery.

Gracie wandered near the buggies and her hand touched one. She spun around facing my direction.

"Small or big buggy?"

I pointed toward the small, gray one.

The perfect size for playing house.

Gracie pushed the buggy up and down the aisle. Elizabeth and I walked in front of her. We placed items from the shelves into the buggy.

Blue ink flowed from my pen onto the white paper. The top of the paper was stamped in gold with my initials.

One-by-one the blue ink slashed each item listed on the grocery list:
tilapia
~~lemon~~
foil
~~broccoli~~
paper towels
milk
eggs
~~spinach~~
chicken broth
~~tea bags~~
~~sweet potatoes~~
~~notecards~~
~~cereal~~
coffee
cheese pizza

Gracie rounded each corner
with the buggy, pushing harder
each time, keeping up with us.
Her small feet stopped in front of
the self-check out.

I paid.

At last, the grocery list and receipt
tossed in the bottom of my purse.

We drove home on our side of the
road.

Out our back door, I stood in
front of the double grill. Seasoned
stuff Tilapia covered the holey
foiled grill tray. Grease sizzled
around the edges of the Tilapia.

Smoke slithered in the air.

Behind it, my attention floated
away.

Flash.

Over and over, flashes of me
looking to my left out my driver
side window. Me looking back
straight ahead. Then out my front
windshield at the road in front of
me. And me realizing my tires
rolling forward in the oncoming
traffic lane.

As the grill closed my feet shuffled
adjacent to the back door.

My thoughts paused.

Could not move.

Stuck.

A sign wedge in the hard ground
of the yard I caught sight of
glancing out my driver side
window.

"Under Contract"

Those two words paused in my head. Under. Contract. More than the swerving of my car. More than seeing the other lane out my front windshield. And more than the food cooking on the open pit.

Meanwhile, Elizabeth pulled four classic drinking glasses from the cupboard beside our stainless refrigerator.

The glassware rested on the painted wood counter top. Her hand grabbed into the freezer behind her. Ice cubes clank in the bottom of each glass.

Gracie's flat-footed stride passes each place setting. She laid out folded, crisp, white napkins and placed a fork on top of each.

Over the years, I have tried to instill how important family mealtime is to my kids.

Even on terrible days.

We don't have many of those, right? Who has those anyways?

The lock on our back door clicked. The door sprung forward. Loud large boots pound up the hallway near the kitchen.

Our family dog barked once.

Shane, my husband, peaked around the corner. At the same time each night he gets home.

Give or take 5 minutes.

He stopped, pushing his leather brown work boots off. One foot. Then the other foot. He sat them next to the cabinet.

Each night, I goo-goo over his handsomeness. Always more than the day before. I build on our love story, daily.

He walked over first.

His whiskers pressed against my cheekbone.

His warm ear pressed against my temple.

Then he grabbed each girl separate, including the dog, snuggle hugging them.

Days before we agreed as a family we'd work on our prayers over dinner.

Hubby's obedient heart prayed.

This has not always been easy for
him, but in God's perfect timing,
the Holy Spirit is moving.

Praying is taking place.

Around our square dining table,
we shined a graceful light on
mastering praying as a family.

Prayers, dinner, clean kitchen and
I tucked both kids into bed.

Shane pulled his desk chair
out.

Then his legs slide under the
cream-colored desk while his
bottom end rest in the striped
chair.

First, he signs his name on
several checks. He then slid each
check in the proper utility
envelope. His tongue licked long
ways, pushing each tab closed.

In the upper left corner of each
envelope, he pushed our circular
return address dispenser.

On each envelope, in the upper
right corner, he stuck postage. His
chair slid back. The envelope
bottoms evenly clicked on the
desk.

He laid the stack of mail on the
end counter. Where we'd know to
mail them the next day.

At last, not missing a beat, his feet
carried him into the living room.
Where I sat in our double size
chair.

In front of the chair, he stopped.
His bottom backed into the chair
next to mine.

I scooted over as much as I could,
without him seeing.

Settled, he snuggled up next to
me, pulling the blanket over his
feet.

We watched the nightly news
together before showering for bed.

Our clean bodies climbed onto our off-white satin sheets, lining our 4-post bed.

"On the way to the grocery store today the kids and I saw an 'Under Contact' sign in the yard of the house on Henderson Street."

Shane's head turned toward mine.

Our eyes met.

"What house? Henderson Street?"

Memorial Day weekend kicked
off the marking of summer.

My Facebook news feed scrolled.

Gradually, my eyes stumble over:

toes covered in sand
a family of four dressed in
crisp white shirts and blue jeans
three teen girls in bikini's
beach-bound statuses
sand buckets
shovels
beach towels
margaritas
ice chest
parasailing
seafood
lifeguards
condos

Until my mouse stopped. I pushed
the keyboard panel forward. Then
my chair slid back. I stood to walk
elsewhere.

My mind squealed.

In that moment, my thoughts stopped. Along with my heart crying out, "Thank you, Jesus, for my family, my friends, for everything, going on in my life and my current location."

"Thank you for no sand in my crack."

By this time, my heart balanced.

Small steps one by one my feet wandered. In front of our double brown front door, they stop.

Across our big green front yard, my eyes gazed. Shane bounced around passing back and forth on his zero turn mower.

Because my season of life calls my family to be home for the holiday weekend, I am overjoyed.

Elizabeth leaves tomorrow for her music mission trip.

Soon the back door burst open.

"Honey."

"Yea."

"I am hungry."

Our feet land in front of each other in the hallway. Sweat rolled off his forehead. His arm pushed up wiping it away. Cheerfully, I scoot an inch closer grabbing the side of his torn gray T-shirt.

"Come shower. Let's go out to dinner?"

Shane turned walking out the back door.

Sounds of his mower perched inside my ears.

The tip of my nose touched the open blind. I watched as he parked his mower under the awning outside our garage.

We ate as a family of four at the local fish house as a great gesture before Elizabeth left town.

Gracie did not gather her cornbread and french fries to feed the ducks.

The three of us, Shane, Elizabeth and I, look at each other. At the same time, we said,

"That's a first!"

Gathering my cell phone and purse, I shift my chair back. Everyone joined. We marched together to the front of the fish house.

Shane paid.

We left.

I watched the ducks swim in the water out my passenger window as we backed away.

Sunday morning we drove to the church for Elizabeth's 6:30 am check-in. On the way there, she shared when she returns she will work intensely on the recycling program for her school.

I leaned back in my seat peering over my left shoulder.

"Wait, what, you will do what?"

Shane's foot continued resting forward on the gas pedal. He pulled in a parking place. The front door was close by.

The four of us went inside the gym.

Elizabeth rolled her big, pink, paisley suitcase behind her. She rolled it by the luggage sign.

We hugged her neck and left.

Wednesday came flying in
sideways. Minus Elizabeth,
several days of quietness settled
in as a pinch of an empty nest.

Gracie and I stood in front of the
mudroom window looking.

Shane pulled his truck next to the
cream flower bucket. Lavender
Lantana draped over the edges.

His headlights shined on our eyes.

He fumbled with an unknown
object on his passenger seat.

The heavy driver side door
opened. In a procrastinating
motion, his feet dangled to a
stance on the pebble concrete.

I took two puny steps back. My
right hand brushed Gracie's left
shoulder.

Shane nudged the back door
open. As Gracie and I
wander to the kitchen.

He walked straight towards the
island. Our take out order
released from his arms.

While he went back to his truck,
Gracie and I fixed three drinks.

When back inside he walked
straight near the island. For the
second time, releasing a cake, ice
cream, flowers and a card.

Under the kitchen sink, I reached
for a glass vase.

Gradually, water flowed from the
faucet. At the halfway mark, water
stopped filling up the sides of the
vase.

Out of the knife block, I grab the
scissors. Over the garbage can, I
trimmed the ends of each flower.

The vase sat in the middle of the
island. Shane reached around my
waist. Against the vase, he rests
the card.

He then leaned into me,
"Happy Birthday."

"I am so sorry I did not tell you this
morning."

We ate.

Shane slipped his hand in the grocery bag sitting on the edge of the counter.

He pulled a pack of white candles out. Then he put them on the cake. Four on one side and three on the other.

And lit them with the lighter torch Gracie pulled from the kitchen draw.

"Happy Birthday to you.
Happy Birthday to you.
Happy Birthday to momma.
Happy Birthday to you.
And many more…"

I blew the candles out.

We ate cake.

We ate ice cream.

Shane stood at the sink.
His back faced me.

The water ran over each dish
while his hand held the smiley
round face sponge scrubbing in
circular motions.

I stood near the island.

Meanwhile, my arm stretched
toward the card. My name is
handwritten on the front.

My hand pulled it near my naval.
Under the edge of the sealed
envelope, my right thumbnail
pushed.

My thumb worked from one side to
the other, I pulled the card out of
the open envelope.

My eyes gleamed.

Tiny turquoise letters covered the front of the white card. On the inside, I peeked, before finishing reading the front.

Shane's handwriting covered the left side. My eyes skipped onto the actual card writing on the right side. On to reading it first.

My eyes wandered back to Shane's handwriting.

His words pumped my heart up in a mighty way. Thanking me for being his wife, being his best friend and for being the mother I am to our children.

The fun mushy stuff everyone wants to hear.

My eyes continued reading to the
bottom where I saw the letters
P.S.

P.S. "Under Contract"

My hands closed the card sliding it
back into the envelope.

Shane's hand pulled the sink lever
down. The water stopped.

He took one step back turning in
my direction. I looked at him. He
looked at me.

His feet took steps
approaching me, while he spoke
up, "Let me explain."

He walked even closer.

"This has been so hard to keep
from you."

"The 'Under Contract' sign you were referring to the other night. The realtor put it on top of the For Sale sign. The day I bought the old Victorian home on Henderson Street for you."

Tears whaled in both of my eyes pushing on to both cheeks.

"Shane!"

"No way!"

I ran to him putting both arms around him.

His arms squeezed me tight.

That night I laid in bed as my eyes
wandered back and forth the
cream ceiling.

A heart full of gratitude, I cried out
to God thanking Him.

My eyes continued pacing, as
extra thoughts formed on and on
around the second home Shane
bought for me to use as my
ART STUDIO.

The clock read 2:33 a.m.
the last time I looked at it.

The next morning, I woke up to Shane standing next to my side of the bed.

As soon as he leaned close kissing my cheek, I whispered, "I love you."

He whispered, "I love you too."

"Have a good day," pushed across my lips.

He plods through the door opening of our room.

When I heard the back door close, I placed both fists beside me pushing myself into an upright posture.

My feet dangled from the side of the bed to a standing position.

I tiptoed to the kitchen pouring a cup of warm coffee.

Next, my hand slipped under the
lampshade in the living space.
Light shined bright on the ceiling
and dim through the room. I
grabbed my Bible and journal from
the edge of the dark, cherry,
coffee table.

My bottom end backs into my
favorite oversize chair.

At this point, I note my thanks, my
gratitude for Shane giving me
such a gift, in my spiral journal.

A few pages back I glance over
my earlier prayers.

Prayers revealing my praying plea
for God to please provide
space for an art studio. A studio
used absolute for His glory.

As a result, this refreshed my
soul. And opened my eyes to His
true goodness.

Praise.

On the edge of the white coffee mug, my lips rest. Sips of warm coffee fill my mouth. Meanwhile, I continue sitting at Jesus' feet. In full communication, I reminisce with Him.

Fill me up Lord, release my control and renew my thoughts.

I want to be well equipped.
I want to have Joy.
I want to have Peace.
I want others to have Joy.
I want others to have Peace.

However, my soul's comforted
knowing no dream or desire of my
heart is too big for His timing.

A big plus on this journey is Shane
is a home remodeling contractor.
He has been one for 15 years.
This gives me hope knowing God
has known of this day. Long
before, I ever dreamed.

My thoughts move fast most days.
Dreams compartmentalized. They
appear comparable to little bitty
clips, picture frames almost. Each
time I am amazed. When I stop
long enough outright thinking, He
is the true creator.

He created me so long ago.

My heart is pitter-pattering. As I realize the truth behind what is taking place in my family's life.

My heart enriches knowing things are taking place so each of us can use our form of art. While we come alive in Him serving others.

Late Friday afternoon, I looked
at my phone, lying on the counter
next to my black fringe purse.
Elizabeth's name popped on my
screen. I swiped my finger across
the bottom of my screen. Then
tapped on Elizabeth's name.

Her message read, *We are back
at the church fixing to eat. I
will see y'all tonight. The concert
starts at 7 o'clock. Be here early
to find a seat. Tell Grammie to
bring a sweater.*

My fingers pressed, *Okay, babe,
we will see you soon.*

An hour before the concert we arrived.

Gracie sat in an end chair. While Shane sat in the opposite end chair. Empty seats between them reserved for family attending.

Elizabeth entered the sanctuary. One of her leaders and three team members walked alongside her.

She turned, looking up at us. Her arm extended in a long distant wave.

I inhaled as fast as I exhaled. A smile on my face.

Her daddy waved at her.

An hour later, her mission team performed in a homecoming concert for friends and family.

One of the neatest things my eyes have ever seen. When one teen moved, 250 made the same move in sync with the music.

The next morning, mid-morning, Shane drove me and the kids on the golf cart to our neighbors house.

They were hosting a graduation party for their son. He was graduating from high school.

The pool was full of teen boys and girls playing games.

Volleyball
Badminton
Corn hull
Basketball
Cards
Headbanz

Crawfish covered our round red trays. I peel them. Naturally, lemonade chased most downward while others drank sweet tea.

Elizabeth said she saw beer in the big yellow cooler.

I played a round of badminton with
two hands full of teens.

One girl stood next to me refusing
to swing her black racket.

She missed every time
haphazardly.

Even her serving did not
harmonize. It was comparable to
watching a white bird land in front
of her.

Cautious she blamed it on the fact
she's left handed.

She was firm in claiming a person
prayed over her in preschool when
she found out she was left-
handed.

Sun beamed on my body.

I turn to the guy next to me. And
hand him my racket. Across the
green grass, my feet carried me.
Under a big red umbrella, I sat in a
black iron chair.

We stayed little longer.

Elizabeth needed to get home to feed the neighbors dog.

Gracie talked our ears off on the ride back home. I told her, "You do not have to yell. We are right here. The neighbors can hear you."

Shane parked the golf cart under the awning next to his garage. "Did you tell Jason we left a graduation gift?"

His answer, "No."

"Please text him. Tell him it is on the end of the kitchen counter. Next to the coffee pot."

Shane looked at me, "Okay." He pulled his phone out of his left front pocket.

Our busy life schedule kicked back off after the weekend. The next time Shane and I spoke of the old Victorian home, we list out our expectations of renovating.

"Having a good plan is always a good start," I told him.

We lay face-to-face in bed. In a verbal manner, we list our dreams of turning the old home into an art studio, non-selfish.

My dream:

name the house
pull up the carpet
have ceiling fans installed in each
room
paint walls a light yellow
clean and dust the entire house
have the wall between dining
and family room knocked out
industrial size sinks
light color tile
a flat slab kitchen countertop
mirror replaced
close the third floor off
apply updates to the second floor
washer and dryer
a nook table
tables lined in dining/family room
for art classes
beds for rooms upstairs
bedding
toilets
towels

Shane's dream:

get the limbs out of the yard
trim bushes
reshape the driveway
paint the mailbox
repaint outside the house
fix the blinds
get boxes off the front porch
fix doorknob on the front door
check air and heat
clean gutters
buff and polish wood floors
check the gas line
check the phone line
check water line to the refrigerator
and whatever Marcy Gene wants

In our square shape laundry
room, I stood facing the washer
against the robin egg blue wall.

Wet clothes touched the palms of
my hands. Each piece of clothing
transferred from washer to dryer
by the tug of my hands.

As each piece passes in front of
me, I pray over them. "Lord, thank
you for my family. Thank you for
entrusting them to my care each
day. Help me to help them to
become more like you. Flood my
home with your presence."

I turned the dryer on.

One foot on the printed rug and
one on the hardwood floor, I then
step back.

Hangers hung on the clothes rod.

Leaning towards the clothes rod, I
take one down. Hang a shirt on it.
After the shirt is on the hanger, I
hung it back on the clothes rod.

The white clothes basket sat on the counter. Towels hung on the baskets edge. The backdoor doorbell rang.

The house slippers on my feet squeaked as I turned toward the door.

Walk.

While my hand rest on the doorknob.

I twist.

Pull.

The door cracked wide enough my two eyeballs could see out.

A man stood with his back facing me. His figure dressed in dark blue overalls and a white T-shirt underneath.

He turned around.

Before making eye contact with me he spoke, "Is your husband home? My wife and I are looking at the house next door."

Our eyes met. I spoke back, "Yes, I'll get him." The back door closed. I turned walking away to find Shane.

I questioned myself, *did he know it was me?*

Shane and I stopped halfway in the long hallway. His eyes squint. His voice utters, "What is it?"

"There's a man at the back door. Said he and his wife are looking at the house next door."

Shane squeezed my upper forearm, "Okay."

Without even asking, What's he want me for, Shane walked on to the back door.

The back door opened, "Hey man."

Shane and I met one Friday
night on the local hangout strip my
senior year of high school. He
tried to court me for over a year
before I gave into a date.

I returned to the laundry room
folding clothes; hearing bits and
pieces of the men talking.

Gracie and Elizabeth walked in
one behind the other. "Who's the
man Dad's talking with outside?"

"Did y'all see through your
bedroom window?"

"Mom!"

My faint voice explains, "The man
said he and his wife were looking
at the house next door."

The back door pushed open.
Shane walked through the door
opening. He turned his head to the
left, looking at me as he kept
walking.

Both kids turned their heads
inwards towards me, looking.

I tossed a beige towel into Elizabeth's hands. In a prompt motion, she tossed the towel into Gracie's hands.

Gracie smashed the towel up tossing it back in the pile.

Both girls ran.

The night was still. My eyes
popped open. Under my pajamas,
my heart raced. The extra
responsibilities owning a second
home raced around in my mind.

What will this bring to my family?

What a large investment Shane
made.

He did not discuss this with me.

I don't want a financial hardship.

The following night before dark,
I sat on the front porch swing next
to Shane.

My hands cupped around my
coffee mug as Shane held the
handle to his mug.

We call this "dating".

As a married mom, I take what I
can.

Shane led our conversations.

"You know Marcy Gene, purchasing the home over renting it will be best."

"Shane, I am worried pertaining the budget strain."

While understanding where I was coming from, he assured me owning the house and property both allowed us to customize things to our liking. We could be flexible matching our taste and needs.

"Permanence," he said.

"When I first looked at the property my dad went with me."

My heart intensely sank deeper…

"Dad and I discussed the location, property taxes, utility, public services, zoning, details of the home and my ability to flip it."

"It was a win, win."

"He and I walked the property over, praying over it, discussing it. When dad's sight beamed in my direction and his words formed saying, 'Son go for it.' Marcy Gene, it occurred God was speaking through my dad."

"I had peace and joy in the moment. Convinced you would too," Shane said as I grabbed his hand looking into his eyes.

"Dad told me to make an offer. I did so knowing he'd provide funds, I'd give funds and the rest from the money your dad left you."

I squeezed Shane's hand tight as tears whaled in my eyes.

"Dad and I had a guy he knows come yesterday to complete the home inspection. Before the sale is complete, a few things will be fixed."

"The title search came back fine. I got homeowners insurance. I told the insurance agent you need to list the belongings, house furnishings etc. He told me that was perfect."

"My attorney's office said once they have the paperwork complete they'd contact me to schedule the closing."

"Who was the guy who came by the other day? The one looking at the house next door?"

I turned my body inward near his. I giggled. My eyes pounced on his while my nose scrunched.

"He said he knew you."
I giggled longer and replied, "He did." "He knew me." "Until, I met you. He was history."
Shane giggled too.

"Are you serious?"

My hand pressed flat against
Elizabeth cream bedroom door. A
slight push, I could see in her
room enough to know she was
sitting on her made bed.

A string of lights shined glares of
bright light here and there
draped across her beige walls.
Her shoulders rolled back into an
upright position. In my direction,
her head turned right. We made
eye contact.

My feet crept closer to her
bedside. When leaning towards
her I whispered, "Good night."

She whispered, "Will you climb
into bed with me? I am working on
the recycling program."

My leg swung into the air, landing
on the edge of her bed. She
slipped her hand out. I grabbed it
in a quick motion. She slung me
on the bed next to her. Everything
in sight on the bed went in the air.

We giggled until tears glazed our eyes. Finally, I got myself together. I told her, "We need to be quiet your sister is sleeping."

Elizabeth acknowledged the fact even though her Headmaster, Mr. Bradshaw, approved the recycle program, each step still needed to be approved by the school board.

The arrow moved on her laptop screen.

While clicking away, she showed me different bin setups, talked of organizing the program and which materials they would use on recycling.

She went over the students who are involved in the program. And even the teacher who'd be helping collaborate the recycling program.

She told me, "You know mom, it's said the teacher will help. I know it's up to us kids. The teacher will only be there to listen if we need anything. We will only hope help is provided. The teachers have so much on them."

My eyes opened hours later
realizing I was still on Elizabeth's bed.

Both hands held her laptop as I slid downward on the edge of her turquoise bedspread. Once my feet touched the carpet, I walked over to her wooden desk sitting her laptop on it.

Passing by her bed, I stopped pulling her chevron print blanket over her.

My left hand slipped over the light switch pushing downward. Then realize it was not the light on. I walked on the other side of her bed unplugging the string of lights. The green cord dropped to the floor next to my feet. At this point, I glance at my feet. I noticed my toenails needed re-polishing.

Tip toeing backward I pulled her door in my direction closing it.

Seven o'clock am the next
morning came, chop-chop.

I hopped out of bed walking over
to Gracie's room.

It was no surprise to her.

She was awake.

This was a day she awaited.

Dressed and ready she roared to
be on the soccer fields.

Her home!

Soccer camp started that Tuesday morning ending Thursday of that same week.

I watched camp coaches work close with Gracie in the goal.

A few years back my heart spun out of control. The more they placed her inside the goal and not on the field.

It was to my surprise God knew the entire time just where He wanted her.

I held on so tight to the field playing time.

When I let go it was HEAVEN on the soccer field for her and I both.

The open hutch on the back of my car blocked the sun from my eyes as I continued watching Gracie.

Her gloved hands moved every possible way in the direction she saw the ball approaching her.

My hand rest next to me on my phone lying on a plaid blanket.

I noticed a small vibration.

Soon looking at my phone, I notice Shane sent a text.

Friday 2 o'clock closing at John Tuckers office off Lena Street.

My phone in my left hand I used my right pointer finger replying with *smiley princess faces, hearts and balloons with confetti.*

Meanwhile, minutes after I laid my
phone back on the blanket
another pulsation of vibration
radiated.

Again, I pull my phone near. By
this time, I notice it was from
Elizabeth.

*I am headed to the school to meet
with the group of students
involved with the recycle program.*

I smiled.

Copying and pasting the same
*smiley princess faces, hearts and
balloons with confetti* from the
message I sent to Shane.

I hit send.

She replied with *a winking smiley
face.*

Gracie tucked her grass stained
gloves in her soccer backpack.

The backpack on her shoulder,
she nods towards a friend. The
friend slipped her hand into the air
waving bye.

Gracie drank water from her water
bottle walking to the car. I stood
closing the hatch on the back of
the car.

We drove away.

Days later, crossing the long
bridge across the water cars
lingered on my front and back
bumper.

Turning, I swished in a dip
entering the driveway at the
attorneys' office.

Two cars from Shane's truck I
pulled in a parking place next to a
brick building.

The kids and I did a mirror check,
grabbed our things and got out of
the car. Shane stood at the
doorway on the porch waiting for
us. As we walked towards Shane,
I hurriedly told Elizabeth and
Gracie they'd need to wait in the
lobby while their dad and I signed
papers.

Shane kissed my cheek and
opened the door for the three of
us.

A lady behind a long desk greeted us. Shane followed up by stating, "I am Shane and this's my wife Marcy Gene."

"Oh, welcome. Have a seat. They will be right with you."

Gracie pushed over in a corner chair with her blue Beats over her ears.

Elizabeth sat next to me asking to hold my keys.

Shane stood peering through the tall slender window.

The same lady from behind the
desk stood in a door opening
calling our name.

I stood grabbing Shane's hand.

I turned back. Quickly, giving both
of the girls "a look".

We walked the long hallway
behind the lady.

"Mr. Tucker will be right with you."

Papers lined along the brown
desk.

Shane pulled a chair out for me.

He sat next to me.

Shane clicked the pen on the table one time before Mr. Tucker walked in the room. Shane pushed his chair back.

He stood extending his hand forward for a gentleman shake.

He then looked my way, "This is my wife…"

I stood. My body frame leaned in facing him. His right hand rested in the air. While, I raised my right arm. My hand slipped in his.

We settled in our seats. Mr. Tucker spoke, "Tell me what you are doing with this property."

"MG is creating an art studio."
"Wow. That's awesome."

He looks at me. In an impressed voice, "How'd you come up with that?" To sum up my thoughts, a joyful response dripped from my lips, "It's been a lifelong passion of mine."

It was small talk from there between him and Shane.

We giggled.

Every time he tapped.

"Sign here."

Due to the original owners living out of town the final walk through and signing papers we did alone.

Once we signed on the last line Shane slid the bank cashiers check across the table in Mr. Tucker's direction.

Mr. Tucker reached inside his brown coat pocket. His hand held the keys to the property. He hands them to Shane.

We pushed our chairs back, standing. Shane leaned towards me. His arm draped hugging my neck. I squeezed him tight. When we pushed back from each other, I looked at his face smiling. "What an achievement."

"When the title releases, a copy will be mailed to you within seven business days," Mr. Tucker stated.

After dinner that night, I sprayed
my homemade essential oils
insect repellent along our front
door.

Long ways on the porch swing my
body relaxed.

After breakfast, the next
morning the four of us, Shane,
Gracie, Elizabeth, and myself
jumped in the Jeep.

We finished our Saturday morning
chores before leaving.

Shane drove us to the paint shop.

Once looking at the paint chips, I
realize color just does something
to my soul.

I love, love, love color.

Over the next several days,
nights and weeks the four of us
along with Shane's work crew
accomplished many things from
mine and Shane's dream list:

dusted, painted, threw trash away,
used brooms, lawn mowers, chain
saws and cleaned windows.

One of those days while
working, Shane was upstairs. I
heard his voice calling me.

It got closer as he stood at the top
of the stepping yelling.

"Marcy Gene."

I stopped the long shop broom in
front of me and hollered, "Yes."

"Remember that cabinet?"

"They left it."

My eyes grew big.

My waist twisted heading to the
bottom of the stairs.

"Are you serious?"
"Bring it here."

"It's real heavy babe."

My Facebook status read, ISO any furniture donations. I am trying to fix up an art studio on Henderson Street. The studio will hold upcoming art retreats for those interested in expressing themselves through fine art.

I posted the same status on my personal page, my Bible study group page and local yard sale pages.

By the end of the third day, the art studio was fully furnished.

Each day for a week, we met for drop off or pickup. It was amazing seeing people step up donating. The stories why they wanted to donate. Or why they did not need that bed or table any longer.

List of donations:

bathroom towels
washer and dryer
a real cute small kitchen table
four different kitchen table chairs
six long tables
twenty-eight metal chairs
three comfy living room chairs
one couch
two small mirrors
four large mirrors
hangers
four bar stools
four beds
a small desk
ottoman
sheets
rugs
clothes basket
pots and pans
dishes
stack of magazines

Elizabeth kept a running list of items donated.

I asked her to get mailing address' when people brought their donations.

In our moments of thoughts, waits, organizing and furthermore settling in Elizabeth helped me write, address and Gracie stamped the thank you card.

After we'd gathered a stack of five or more I'd walk them to the mailbox.

I'd slide the cards in the opened mailbox praying over each one.

So thankful for God's generous people, giving.

There were days we needed
time away from the studio to keep
up the home we presently owned.

Shane pulled our camper out,
pulling the sheets, blankets,
towels, dishes, pots and pans out.

He scrubbed every single inch
inside and out, top to bottom.

Sounds of dishes crashing came
from my kitchen. I walked in
looking at him.

As a result, I kept my mouth shut.

No words. In the laundry room, I
realized the towels and bedding
from the camper lying on the floor.

My heart raced. The fact, I
emptied the laundry room from our
normal laundry load earlier.

Believe me, I did not ask
questions. Nor said a word.

Later, I heard him calling the camper lodge. He questioned their help in selling it.

When he went back outside, I put my yellow flip flops on and followed him.

Through the rays of sun, my eyes glazed. I said, "You did it, huh? You know I could post it on the Facebook yard sale page."

He looked at me with a smirk on his face.

"It's just time, time for a change."

I smiled back.

Before the day was over we got the JR. dirt bike, 2 WD 4 wheeler and two bicycles out. We cleaned them, took pictures, and I posted them sitting right there.

As time goes on, it feels so good to turn loose of things and move forward, reframing from hoarding tendencies.

By night, we had four inquiries on the camper.

Elizabeth and I sat around the dining room table sorting puzzle pieces by color.

Yesterday, we formed the outer edge pieces. We chat canvassing the art studio while sorting.

"Mom, when the art studio is finished, what will be my job description?" This I confirmed, "You know Elizabeth, I am not fully sure. We will have to get in there. Then I'll let you know. What I need from you now is help naming the studio."

Another puzzle piece slipped in place. My heart poured out the vision for the studio.

Elizabeth looked into my eyes.

A grin was on her face.

My vision:

A fun fluffy place for women to come. A space where they can allow themselves to shine and know they are already amazing. A place to relax. Get away from the fast pace outside world-let go of the world. Be free.

Near the same time, the next morning Gracie and I awake.

A coffee mug rest in my palms. Her medium size hand pulled a coffee mug from the cabinet next to the refrigerator.

She filled hers with cocoa.

Her head peeked in my direction. "Do we have marshmallows?"

"Go to the pantry", I told her. "Look on the right-hand side. Near the middle."

Once she completes making her cocoa. She wanders in the dining room. Next to me she sits in the chair.

We cupped our hands around our mugs. As if it were freezing. We sipped our hot drinks. It was dead of summer, 90 degrees.

In that moment, I pulled the light color matchbox blinds up.

We sat looking at the unfinished puzzle. However, not one piece was placed in yet for the morning.

A car motor hummed by.

Through the door window, I saw a dark box shape older car. It putted past our house. My body stood. In the window, I lean forward investigating.

My eyes glued to the car, I watch as it made its way into the cul-de-sac.

With enough time, I pushed my left leg back as my foot rest on the square print rug. My hips make a slight turn. As I leaned over to the table, I set my coffee down.

Both feet slid towards the door again. I looked hard watching the car pass my house again.

It stopped at the house diagonal from mine. It was the "trash" lady again.

Elizabeth was still asleep.

She is the one who told us of the "trash" lady. Only she put it to us, "We have a trash digger."

When you see things with your own eyes it makes it that much more real.

This was real.

The "trash" lady got out walking around the back of her car where the trash sat on the edge of the yard.

The tree brush line blocked the majority of my view. In a sudden movement, she dashed back into her car.

Her wheels rolled forward.

Gracie's jaw flopped open.

The next time the girls and I
drove to the art studio, we carried
our ENO hammocks.

Shane told me his work week will
be busy. So his time's limited
helping at the studio.

The time ended up being perfect.

It gave us girls time to familiarize
ourselves with everything.

We could not wait to have classes.

For the meantime, we worked on
the things we could without
Shane's help.

Often we took breaks, lying in our
hammocks tied among the trees
out back.

Back inside the girls and I were lining the tables with brown paper.

We heard someone knock on the door. Elizabeth walked over glancing out the window. She looked back at me, "It's dad's workers."

My heart dropped.

Elizabeth's hand covered the brass doorknob. She pulled the door open towards her.

In front of the door was a younger gentleman dressed in a plaid shirt and jeans. One we did not recognize. "Your dad told us to come on over here and start on some things outside until he gets here."

Elizabeth's face lit up, "Oh, okay, great."

When Elizabeth shut the door, she
turned looking at Gracie and I.
"Mom, he's hot, real hot."

Gracie's lower lip did a weird
thing, squeezing out "eww."

In no time, I heard the front door
of the studio open again.

I walked towards the front window
pushing the curtain to the slight
left with the backs of my fingertips.

Both of Elizabeth's hands grasp
the top of the long mirror propped
against the front porch wall.

In a sliding motion, she pulled the
mirror towards herself as she
walked backward.

The unfamiliar young worker gentleman ran up behind her.

"Hey, hey let me help you."

"Oh, thank you. Mom said she does not want to keep it. It's been here since we bought this place. Can you help me carry it to the trash pile around back?"

"Sure."

They both grabbed an end of the mirror as he leads backward on the steps. She followed in his direction moving forward on the steps.

In a sideways motion, walking in the grass, they both held the mirror carrying it to the back of the property.

When Elizabeth came back inside, Gracie and I stood working on putting supplies into the vintage cabinet Shane brought from upstairs.

Elizabeth was so giddy.

I told the girls we needed to go home for the day.

We loaded up in the car.

Elizabeth told me the young gentleman's name at the door was Noah.

"He said, he's been working for dad a few weeks."

"He touched my hand."

The following day, the girls and
I took a day trip to my mother's
two hours away.

Gracie was glad to sleep in before
we hit the highway. The last two
mornings she got up early. She
went to work with her dad.

I am true in believing in every little
girl's life they want to spend time
at work with their dad.

When we made it to mom's house,
she informed us details
concerning her appointment with
her diabetic doctor.

We played the game Clue and ate
tuna salad.

We visited and laughed.

At 4:00, it was time to head home.
A busy day was ahead for the next
day.

Dinner. Bedtime. Alarms set.

What a special day.

We sat under a breezy awning towards the corner. I began people watching. The oversized fans blew through our hair. Once we got situated. It was just right.

The bride and groom, my best friends daughter, entered the wedding reception from one of the outside entrances.

Shane stopped along the way talking to several of his customers.

The band played.

TV's lined the outer edges of the awning. The world cup covered the screen.

Elizabeth spotted a man who dipped in the drinks too much. He wobbled as he sat in his chair, at a table with his friends.

Everything was so Southern.

I leaned in towards Shane's ear
telling him to run back to the car
for their gift basket.

He sat it on the long table pushed
against the front wall. Everyone
stopped looking at it. I guess you
could say it was Pinterest looking.

Big, fluffy, beige towels rolled up
lined the back of the
oversize brown laundry basket.
Tossed in front of those were
laundry accessories:

clothes soap
clothes pins
softener
borax
dryer sheets
handmade laundry room sign
iron
small iron board
starch
clothes bag
the grandma's secret spot
remover

I made a card from an old cereal box for them. Acrylic white paint covered the box. Then I folded it in half. On the front of the card, I glued a cutout watercolor painting by me, of a bride and groom.

Inside the card were strong handwritten words of encouragement that most never hear of marriage.

There will be good days, lots of them, there will be okay days, a few, there will be not so okay days, many. Each of those days start with your maker, first and for most. Not only the bad days.
Not only the okay days.
Not only the good days.
Each one of them.
His love is greater than anyone else's. He will fill you up, equipping you daily for each task at hand.
Don't depend on or rely on the other to do this tasks only He can.

I sealed the card with a kiss.

Elizabeth presented me with a handmade ticket out of cardboard early the next morning.

The ticket stated the name she chose for the art studio.

Letters painted in coral on top of a white background spelled out "Fancy Faith".

"Oh Elizabeth, I love it."

"How perfect is that…"

"Thank you so much."

Tears streamed my face. One by one, things fell into place. A few hurdles and hoops here and there but favorably came together.

The name of the studio came at the perfect time. The title came in, classes were on the schedule and the yard sign was in the making.

However listening to the heart
of Gods people can take you on
walkways you did not see coming.

I received an email from a lady
who was Shane's customer. She
inquired the upcoming art studio.

Her daughter's in first grade and
she is looking for classes for her.

It's funny how things come at the
perfect time. Just days before my
heart was thinking of scheduling
special class times for kids.

This is when I saw my vision for
the studio changing.

Elizabeth went to volleyball
camp. Gracie went with her.

I worked at the studio between my
duties at home. My daily job
reminds me what to keep first:
My husband,
My kids,
My home,
My family.

The camper sold to a precious
little family.

Elizabeth's was at a product full
state with the recycling program.

Father's Day came and went.

We saw the "trash" lady again.

A soccer coach tried to recruit
Gracie for his team.

Shane told Elizabeth more on his
worker, Noah.

I received a thank you card from
the wedding gift.

One morning at home, the doorbell rang.

Gracie and I looked at each other.

A long scan of beeps pounds in my ears. In a whispering voice, I told Gracie, "It must be UPS."

We watched the driver run back to his brown box truck. There he wiped his sweaty head with a white towel. He never looked our way.

Gracie opened the door pulling the box towards her. She ran to the kitchen, grabbing the scissors. After walking back, she knelt beside the boxes. Once the top sliced open, she pulled the packaging out.

I saw the packing list and asked her to check it.

Minutes later, she reported back. We have two extra items and one missing.

My phone was sitting next to the calendar stretched out across the round kitchen table.

It vibrated.

I finished writing the words 'art retreat' before I checked my phone.

Ronnie, my best friend's name popped up on my screen. Her short text read, "Call me." My pointer finger tapped the blue "messages" word on the upper left of my screen. Then, my thumb, in a firm motion pushed my home button carrying me back to my home screen.

I laid my phone back next to my calendar.

Elizabeth walked through expressing two of her friends were coming over that night. She requested them to help paint the bar stools bright orange for the studio.

As I uncluttered the table, I punched in Ronnie's number on my keypad. In front of my kitchen window, I stood looking at two large hawks sitting in the tops of the trees in our backyard.

Last night, Shane said, "They must be mating." Side by side, we stood looking. He let me look through his camo binoculars first. Then he looked through them.

Ronnie's voice said, "Hello." Not a simple hello, but a long drawn out

h e l l o.

One that sounded as if lots of tears flowed before saying it.

Gracie walked by reminding me, "Wear bug spray tonight." I nod.

"Ronnie!" "I know Mary Gene." "It's Jago!" "What, is he okay?"

"He told me I was not moving with him."

"What do you mean?" "He wants a divorce." "What, no way Ronnie?"

Ronnie and I talked for a long time. I confess to her I never dream she'd be calling me with this news. I figured she wanted to chat on the newlyweds, her daughter.

Ronnie and Jago have been lifelong friends of ours. Shane will be hurt for sure over this.

It's a death.

Divorce is a death.

It's not fair.

It affects so many people. Not just the people who walk away from each other.

Dear Lord please, please wrap your arms around Ronnie and Jago. Allow their hearts to be open to you, your understanding, your guidance, and your counsel. May they seek your face first. Let their spirit/faith grow as they walk through this hardship. I pray too for their families, their friends, their kids and anyone whose pavement of future is involved. Thank you, Lord, for making me available for Ronnie. Amen.

"Thank you, Marcy Gene, I could sense His presence."

We got off the phone. I Dialed Shane's number.

"Hello"

"Sounds as if you are busy. Can you talk for a second?"

"I can't Marcy Gene. Can it wait?"

"Sure, I'll see you tonight. I love you."

"Love you."

Shane and I met for a nighttime
meal at the local fancy sandwich
shop. Shane saw Elizabeth's first
pediatrician. He walked over to
him, called out his name, "Dr.
Swan" and shook his hand.

Everyone at Dr. Swan's table
looked from that direction my way.

My right hand slipped in the air.
While smiling, I waved.

Everyone including his wife waved
back. Another couple sat with
them.

Our table number was 67.

Shane got a turkey sandwich with
no honey mustard. And I got a
simple salad, but man was it
large?

Not much simple.

Creamy ranch covered each piece
of lettuce.

Over dinner, I told Shane Ronnie text me earlier that day. "She requested I call her." Then I blurt it out,

"Ronnie and Jago are getting a divorce."

He turned to his right looking at me. Puzzled. "What?" slipped across his lips.

Out of the corner of my mouth, I squeezed a faint, "I know." I slide my left hand towards him and rubbed the outer edge of his upper right arm.

"I talked to him this week."

We finished sipping on our drinks and headed over to get Shane's haircut. We walked in the barbershop. Shane wrote his name on the sign in list.

"Shane"

I continued looking at the
magazine I grabbed from the table
next to me. Now and then I'd look
up seeing the lady barber running
the clipper from bottom to top,
comparable to how a lawn mower
trimmed.

Shane walked towards me. I
stood. We walked out the door
next to me.

Our next stop was the lawn shop.

Then we stopped at the gas
station. Shane pumped gas in my
car and his. Then we drove home.

The kids were home by then.

Elizabeth was serving as a team
leader for the week while Gracie
engages in a sports group at
vacation Bible school.

My heart led me to wait until the
next day to tell the kids Ronnie
and Jago were divorcing.

Life can throw such curve balls.
We have to catch them holding to
God's truth, strength and move
forward.

Mom constantly says,

"No one's perfect."
"No one's life is pure."
"No one's spousal relationship is
perfect."

I used to not realize it,
but now-a-days I do.

Mom is right!

No one is perfect.

I will not lie, I am upset Ronnie and Jago's marriage didn't last. I'll say it again divorce is DEATH.

Some make it and some DON'T.

It's been two weeks since Ronnie, told me.

Not only have I prayed for Ronnie, but I have reached out praying for Jago too.

Him not responding to my text, but I know God is.

It hurts sometimes.

At this point, I fully lay it before the Lord.

Surrender.

Trust.

A traveler's life is always
comprised of two days spent
traveling: one day to get to your
destination one day return to
where it begins. Then pulling
away, heading back, "back to
reality" as most say. It's during
those tangible moments between
those two days you unwind and
your heart, mind, body and soul
skips to a different beat.

The change of
sound
lights
music
pace
people
language
streets
drivers
food
sight

Those moments are what I am to experience watching others experience those moments coming to the studio.

This coming weekend is opening weekend, the first art retreat of the year.

The first art retreat in my art studio…

"A Different Beat"

July 25-27
3-day art retreat
with Mary Gene Wonders

Come spend two nights and three days along with Marcy Gene in her art studio. First floor's designed for studio space with a nook/kitchen that sits towards the back of the floor plan. The second floor is complete room and lodging quarters with two full baths. The third floor is yet to be decided, unfinished.

$350

Friday-You are ART
1-2 arrival/unpack
2-5 class
5-7 dinner/free time
7-9 class assignments

Saturday-In the MIDDLE
9-11 class
11-1 lunch/free time
1-4 class
4-7 dinner/free time
7-9 class assignments

Sunday-Come ALIVE
9-11 class
11-1 lunch/free time
1-2 pack up
2 leave for home

You are ART

Please bring scraps of paper from your home: receipt, napkin, clothes tag, sticker, stamp, printed paper, book page, tea bag wrapper, oatmeal packaging, etc. Any paper found in your day-to-day life bring it in a gallon size Ziploc bag.

You will use these scraps of paper creating. We will create and discuss how we were created to make art. Whether we use our hands signing, being a mom, mentoring someone, traveling or decorating your home we make art.

In the MIDDLE

It's in the day-to-day life we see, hear, smell and touch those things around us. What I call the middle moments. In those Middle moments our hearts, mind, body, and soul take in so much that if we relax taking it in we skip a beat. Our bodies long to receive comfort.

Come ALIVE

Once we have received the
comfort our bodies long for and
we are aware with brave hearts,
confident hearts. We come alive
releasing our art into the world for
the next person to experience life.

Be who you are…
Don't hinder yourself…

You're created to make art, Come
ALIVE.

Directions:

Fancy Faith's is located at
1564 Maple Drive
Brandon, MS 39047

Approx. 12 miles from the airport
Approx. 8 miles from interstate 20
Approx. 3 miles from Hwy 25

Lodge/Housing:

Fancy Faith is a complete art
studio and lodging headquarters.
4 bedrooms/two twin beds each
and 2 full baths on the second
floor. On the lower floor is the art
studio space along with a half
bath, laundry room (wash/dryer
available), a nook/kitchen space.

Registration:

$350

This includes 2-nights 3-day stay with art classes, breakfast, lunch, and a snack. Supplies are provided. Although I ask you bring paper scraps (see good to know section) spaces limited.

Refunds:

All fees required in advance with no refunds. (I know emergencies happen, please let me know)

Good to know:

Fancy Faith has seating, chairs, tables, hammocks, out back for lounge time. Bedding is provided. Laundry supplies provided. Kitchen utensils provided along with food for breakfast, lunch, dinner and a snack. Art supplies provided, except I ask you to bring scraps of paper… gum wrappers, napkins, map, book pages, tea bag wrapper. Watch for things you put in the trash daily. If you have a favorite art supply please bring, but be mindful of limited space.

Contact:

Marcy Gene Wonders
fancyfaith@yahoo.com
P.O. Box 1012
Brandon, MS 39047

By Thursday night before the
first art retreat, all slots available
were full expect one.

I was okay with that!

Friday morning Shane worked his normal hours. Because of this the girls, Gracie, and Elizabeth came to the studio with me. We finished preparing for guest to arrive.

As calm as a girl could be, I stood as a charm. In that final hour, awaiting everyone's arrival. A simple silent prayer pressed through my veins, asking God to use me, fill me up, let me be your light through the work taking place.

I heard a lite knock on the front door of the studio. My thoughts rushed to someone's early.

The front window curtain pushed opened by a nudge of my hand. Enough to see on the other side of the door.

A lady dressed in light color jeans with a yellow plaid shirt, draped over the belt loops, stood there.

Quick, I opened the door towards me. The lady's voice traveled calmly but loud. She stated, "I live two doors over. My name is Chynna." "Oh, hi I am Marcy Gene."

We chat a few minutes. Then Mrs. Chynna headed back to her house ten acres over. She returned home to pack her bags.

I'll be the first to admit, I am happy to say, I offered her the last spot available for the retreat. Although she was hesitant in taking me up on the offer. There is no doubt,

I saw a sparkle in Mrs. Chynna's eyes!

Soon, a small taxi van pulled in the drive. Two ladies slid out. I walked out the front door.

One reached into the backseat for something while the other one waved smiling at me.

"Welcome ladies, can I help you with your things?"

Their feet shuffled closer. As bags filled their arms, "We have everything."

Elizabeth stood in the doorway, "Welcome y'all. We are so glad you are here." She motioned up the stairway, " You can put your stuff upstairs. Pick a room. Any room. You two are the first here. So you get the first pick."

When I walked back into the doorway, Elizabeth and I looked smiling at each other.

She knew my dream for the studio.

In those moments, we both watch everything come alive. My eyes continued peering deep into hers. She states the oblivious,

"God is good."

Feet scuffled on the floor above us. Several cars pull in the driveway. Elizabeth and I continue our greeting.

Gracie jiggled the last set of paintbrushes into the Folgers coffee can. Then she joined us.

You could see the smile in her heart too.

This movement witnessing my daughters receive God's true love, knowledge, wisdom and experiences mean the world.

Their closeness working with me through this showed they don't have to go far from home to find happiness, joy, meaning contentment in this life.

As long as God is first while walking in obedience, He will brighten your path. The growth might have been slow, but each of us stood in faith.

I glanced at my phone. A
message appeared on the screen.
Shane, "Good luck baby!" My
heart melted.

Once everyone settled in they made their way downstairs.

In the kitchen a snack waited on the open bar. "Please make yourself at home. Grab a snack and let's head into the studio."

People mingled.

When I saw it fitting, once everyone spoke to each other and grabbed a fast pinch of snack, I introduced myself.

I am so glad each of you come to spend the weekend with us.

My name is Marcy Gene and these are my girls, Elizabeth, and Gracie. They will help us throughout the weekend. So please if you need anything let one of us know.

My husband, Shane, pops up from time to time so don't let it alarm you.

I can't tell you how much this means seeing my first art retreat taking place. It feels so natural. Virtually, as if I have been doing it forever.

I am so blessed to have each of you as the chosen ones to be here experiencing the start of this studio.

God has great plans for you and I this weekend. So please, please relax and enjoy yourself.

Now if we could go around the table and introduce yourself. Give us a description of yourself:

where you're from
have you ever been to an art retreat
a synopsis of your art history

I'll go first.

Again, my name is Marcy Gene. I am from Mississippi and grew up in Clinton 40 miles from here. This is my first ever art retreat. Not just me hosting, but I have never been to one. I have seen, heard and read of them but never attended one. I have taken online classes. And even taught an online class. My major in college was fine arts. When I graduated, it was hard to find work. So I ended up working in the billing cycle department at the gas company. The pay was good. It got the bills paid and kept me on my feet. Shane and I met, married and had kids. I came home working towards where I am today.

Anyone like to go next!?

The lady on my right squirmed
one time in her seat. Then she
stretched words,

"I am Jeni Lynn. I live in Athens,
Ohio where I was born and raised.
My entire family lives there. Art
runs in my family. So I have
doodled in it off and on my whole
life.

I thought coming around like-
minded people would be a fun
way to spend the weekend.

This is my first retreat to attend."

*Thank you, Jeni Lynn, I love that,
two names. We are so glad you
are here with us.*

When Jeni Lynn got quiet, I looked around to see if anyone else was ready to go next.

The lady sitting across from Jeni Lynn slipped her hand up just below her shoulder.

I nodded towards her.

"My name is Casey.

My family and I live in Monroe, Louisiana."

Monroe, nice Casey, thank you for introducing yourself. Do you have any background in art?

"No!"

My eyes bounce around the room as I smile nodding in Casey's direction.

Before I could speak the lady next to Casey spoke.

"My name is Rosie.

I am Jeni Lynn's sister-in-law. So, I too live in Athens, Ohio. My husband is Jeni Lynn's brother. We grew up together. I don't consider myself as an artist. Maybe a creator, doer of things fun, full of life, bring life to everything around my family and I. I have accompanied one other art retreat.

It was a local retreat."

Wow, Rosie, thank you.

Everyone relaxes the more they hear others talking and telling their story.

When Rosie finished the lady across from her spoke. Somewhat in her seat, she fidgets bumping Jeri Lynn's elbow.

They both grabbed their elbows at the same time.

"I am so sorry.

My name is Harper. I am from Hamilton, Alabama. My grandparents raised me there. This is my 3rd art retreat to attend and I am super pumped to be here."

Fun, Harper, thank you.

On the other side of Jeni Lynn, a soft little voice uttered,

"I am Summer.

I live here. Born and raised in Mississippi. I have never attended an art retreat before but love, love art.

My best friend knows Marcy Gene. That's how I heard details of the retreat."

I smiled at Summer.

Then my eyes slid onto Mrs. Chynna. She shook her head side to side looking at me.

I spoke on her behalf.

Y'all this is Mrs. Chynna.

I pointed my arm towards her with my palm opened upward. As I spoke of her, she smiled.

An hour before guest arrived she knocks on my door introducing herself. She lives on this road.

When I mentioned the art retreat, her face lit up. So, I invited her to come.

"Have you been to an art retreat before Mrs. Chynna?" Her chin nodded up and down.

Oh fun, well we are so glad you are with us today.

After everyone's introduced, I encouraged them to get their scrap paper out.

Some had theirs packed neat in a Ziploc bag, in an envelope, open stacks and some even returned to their bags upstairs to gather theirs.

Elizabeth passed out 12x12 sheets of watercolor paper.

Class, I picked a watercolor paper for the thickness vs. the fact they are watercolor.

Small, little, silver aluminum ashtray's sat in front of each person. I found the trays on a dollar wrack.

Elizabeth poured Mod Podge in each one.

Words of mine formed, instructing everyone to spread as many pieces of paper they could out on the sheet of paper.

146

Go with what feels good. You've got to have a crystal mind. Think of things that are true, honorable, right, pure, lovely, admirable excellent and praiseworthy.

I pulled my scraps from a side
box. Then slid a piece of
watercolor paper in front of me.

My hand ran across the flat paper,
as my mind geared up for placing
my scraps, where they "felt good".
Everyone watched as I continued
showing the featured piece.

With every piece of scrap slid into
place, words traveled along the
sides of my cheeks, as my tongue
pushing them out of my mouth.

Words to the effect of us being
created to make art.

Not everyone understands art.
Not everyone recognizes art.

Momma always said, "There's no
money in art."

Guys, I am here to tell you, it's not the money, it's what gift God gave us to lavish the great Kingdom of His.

When we get knee deep, face down, and come to terms with the greatness of His love. We grab hold to what He's blessed us with, that's art!

We are ART!

The artist created us, we are His masterpiece and what He puts in front of us is His creation we must fluff up, bring to life!

If we are:

cooking
being a mom
traveling
singing
mentoring
decorating your home
bird watching
helping at VBS
helping with prom
tending to your aging dog
seeing to your elder parents
house sitting for someone
being respectful
making healthy choices
cooking a meal for your mate
doing laundry

You get it!?

What we are doing right in front of us every day is art.

It's not just in the paint!

So momma's right, again!

There's no money in art.

No one paid Him to create us and there forth, no one is paying us to create in our everyday life.

Have fun, live life, create ART!

We are ART!

I am ART!

YOU ARE ART!

My spill was complete as I finished placing Mod Podge on each scrap that fell in place.

I held the paper in the air after I paste the last scrap. At last allowing everyone to see how it turned out.

While encouraging them to continue on with theirs, I asked them to reflect on their own life as they paste each piece into place.

Class wrapped up in time for a
dinner break.

Everyone gathered in the kitchen.
Elizabeth and Gracie had
everything set out for us.

Would anyone bless our food?

Everyone took one step back.

The Spirit prompt me, *Lord, we praise you. We sing praises each day of our life over your name. Jesus. Be with us when we may fail. Help us see we are art. Allow confidence to rein over our life. It is easy to be weak. It is easy to think we cannot do things. We know it is through your strength and your perfect love we can press on overcoming obstacles to walking out the purpose you have for our life. Lord, I pray for each of these ladies as they are here for the weekend. May a renewing of your spirit form strengthen their hearts in a leap of growth. Allow them to enjoy time in your presence. Allow them to hear your voice speaking over their life. Oh Lord, help me deliver things the way you would have me to throughout the rest of this weekend. Bless this food to the nourishment of our bodies. Amen.*

After eating, I excused myself.

Y'all meet me back in the studio at 7.

I walked out on the porch.

I breathed in.
I breathed out.
Repeatedly.

My shoulder rest on the
slender pole next to me as my feet
dangled along the brick facing of
the porch.

I heard a lite tap on the window
next to me. At this point, I
turn around. My eyes cut across
seeing Gracie looking at me.

While using her pointer finger, she
motioned for me to come back
inside.

My feet shuffled towards the door.

Everyone sat back in their original seats around the tables in the studio.

As I stood at the end of the table, I shared details of our night-time exercise.

Smiles slide across everyone's face.

The exercise performed by the entire group formed lots of laughter in the room.

When class was over everyone pushed their chairs back.

I walked towards Summer extending my arm to hug her.

Our bodies pushed back from each other. She thanked me for class so far, "I am enjoying this!"

Everyone else mingled among each other.

Elizabeth and Gracie grabbed their bags. We excused ourselves and let them know we'd be back in the am.

Please make yourself at home!

I'll be back at 8 am for breakfast.

My car wheels rolled us into our
home driveway.

The girls grabbed their belongs
heading in the back door towards
their beds.

My things settled in as I pushed
each shoe off at the back door.

Shane was awake. I showered
and told the girls good night.

Shane and I lay in bed discussing
our days. "Tell me more," he
muffled along the edge of his
feather pillow.

My eyes grew heavy.

Peeps of the sun crept through
the edges of the bedroom window.

A bird sat on our fence, chirp,
chirp, chirp, chirp…

Shane's elbow nudged in my side.
My feet swung from the bed
landing firm on the carpet. I could
hear Shane's feet do the same.

After showering for the day, I tip
toe towards the girls bedrooms.
Smells of fresh shampoo touched
the edges of my nose upon
reaching their bedrooms.
Elizabeth's bedroom light shined
under her door.

I nudged Gracie's side. Her eyes
opened. She showered. Dressed.
Grabbed her bag. Elizabeth
grabbed her belongings.

I kissed Shane goodbye. He
walked behind us, "Girls have a
good day. Help mom. Dad loves
you."

Worship music drifted from the car door speakers as my car wheels rolled forward around the corner.

The front door pushed forward as Elizabeth's hand laid on the doorknob. She walked through the door opening first.

We made our way into the kitchen where we helped each other whip up muffins.

Noises scrambled above our heads.

We prepared the drink space with water bottles, apple juice boxes, and orange juice boxes.

My hand reached turning the kitchen radio on low. Sounds from the local Christian radio station played.

The ladies from upstairs walked to the bottom of the stairs one-by-one and staggering small groups.

I did a head count.

One was missing.

I wait a minute keeping the count to myself.

The handheld timer went off. I reached for my oven mittens. Slip my hand in the mitten. Then I opened the oven pulling the muffin pans out. One-by-one, I sat them on the stovetop.

A butter knife wedged each muffin out one-by-one onto a platter.

I motioned for Elizabeth to let them know everything was ready.

My right hand pointing long ways touched the tip of the counter next to me, *Plates are over here.*

We have coffee on this end of the counter, my left hand dangled towards the coffee. *On the other side of the coffee pot, you will find water, apple juice, and orange juice.*

I heard footsteps on the stairs.

Rosie entered the kitchen.

She and I made eye contact. She walked towards me, "I am fine my husband called. We have a sick child and we were trying to work through it."

I placed my arm on hers, *I am sorry girl, thank you for letting me know. I'll be praying for you. Keep me posted.*

She smiled looking into my eyes,
"Thank you, that means so much."

*Sure, I knew someone was
missing from our group. I
was coming upstairs to check.*

My feet walked three steps back,
*Okay ladies, did everyone sleep
well? Does anyone need anything.*

Everyone chuckled and smiled.
One slid their chair back as,

"I am fine."
"Everything was great for me."
"Good sleep."
"I am so thankful to be here."

mashed together.

Let's bless the food.

*When you're finished eating meet
me at the art tables.*

Back at the art tables I mentioned, *Y'all, remember the first thing we worked on yesterday with the paper scraps?*

We will use those again today.

Next to the table where everyone sat in their same seats as yesterday, I stood holding the stack of watercolor art pieces.

One-by-one, I held them up to see if each person could recognize their own sheet.

Who's is this?

Everyone somewhat knew which one was theirs.

A few I turned over checking the backs for a name.

*Okay, now everyone has theirs.
Let's talk for a minute. Run your
hand across the tops of them
while they lay flat in front of you.*

*Notice the texture, the lumps,
bumps, shapes, and sizes of the
scrap papers and mod podge.
Imagine those as your life.*

*We want a smooth life, but it's fact
there will be texture along the
way. When we know this,
experience this, recognize this it
makes us aware of the elegance
held in the lumps and bumps.*

*Now, align your hands flat in the
middle of your page.*

Once you have them there kinda keep track in your head where they are and use a sharpie from the carousel trays in front of you to trace each hand.

The hands on the paper represent

IN THE MIDDLE

of life.

Most leaned forwarded grabbing a black sharpie. When I realized Mrs. Chynna was looking around the room. Her eyes gazed out the window next to her.

The rest of the ladies talked among themselves as this task was under way.

I turned my back to place my sheet of paper on the small table next to me.

A small movement at the back of the table caught my eye. I looked close. A small black spider crept.

My right hand grabbed a white tissue from the box next to me. I laid the tissue over the spider. At last, I grab the spider. Naturally, I glance out of the corner of my eyes. I checked, check to see if anyone noticed. The tissue smooched tight in my hand. Under the table, I dropped it in the trash.

My focus gained back on course. I noticed Mrs. Chynna still not tracing her hands.

I eased closer to her. Then, I leaned in mumbling, *Do you need something Mrs. Chynna?*

Her eyes gazed up at me. Tears whaled along her lower lid. My hand slid on her shoulder.

Are you okay?

Her feet forced her chair away from the table. As she stood up walking towards the front door, I followed her on the front porch.

When I closed the door behind
me, a truck passed by on the
street in front of the studio. A
straw blower was attached to the
truck.

A man dressed in a red t-shirt
stood on the green straw blower.
Hay flew fast through the air
landing on the dirt space.

Pipe work was performed earlier
in the week.

Mrs. Chynna and I look at each other.

So, what's going on Mrs. Chynna?

In this moment, she picked at her nails. While looking at the ground she admits, "The exercise makes me think of something's in my life."

Really? I replied. *How so?*

Her head lifts looking across the yard, "I haven't talked to my daughter in years."

Wow, Mrs. Chynna. Thank you for telling me that.

"Yeah. I passed her on the street the other day."

Really?, pushed from my lips as I moved closer to her.

Mrs. Chynna earned her space. So, I kept my distance. Both my hands rest on the brownish pole column next to me.

I have a question for you Mrs. Chynna.

Our eyes meet.

Do you know Jesus Christ as your Lord and Savior?

Still looking at me she replied, "Yes, yes I do."

I smiled at her.

Can I hug you Mrs. Chynna?

She leaned in towards me.

I slipped my arm around her back giving her a side hug.

Here's what I know Mrs. Chynna. God did not send you here to this retreat by mistake. He is mighty to save us. I am in complete aw to be a part of your story this far in your journey. He has great plans for your life. You can count me as your sister in Christ for life. I will pray for you. Not only today, but in the upcoming days. May you listen as He speaks to you. And you will know it's him. May He guide and direct you to restore the relationship between you and your daughter.

Now, let's get back inside and finish this project.

We both walk toward the door. I stopped. My head turned looking over my left shoulder.

You can push through this. He will heal you. Let's watch His hand at work.

My right hand pushed the door.
While my left turned the doorknob.

Mrs. Chynna followed me.

She walked over to her seat.

I looked at everyone's work.

Wow, guys everyone's work is looking great.

Thanks for y'all's patience while Mrs. Chynna and I talked.

She's at a crossroad in her life.

She could use our prayers.

I grabbed a black sharpie.

Mrs. Chynna, do you want me to trace your hands?

Without saying a word, she lifts both of her hands placing them on her scrap page in front of her.

I traced the left one first.

Mrs. Chynna are you left or right handed?

She wobbled her right hand in the air as I continued tracing the left one.

Oh, neat. Right handed!

I looked up at everyone else, *Y'all can go to lunch. I will be a few minutes.*

Mrs. Chynna and I kept working on her project while everyone else pushed their chairs far away from the table gathering their things for lunchtime.

I heard Elizabeth telling everyone, "The food should be here soon."

The doorbell rang. Elizabeth walked in a fast swaying motion.

Her hand hovered over the doorknob. Gradually, she pulled it towards her.

The delivery guy was polite speaking as Elizabeth motioned towards the kitchen where she knew the meals should be placed.

I sprint towards them to help place the food in the perfect location.

He handed me the receipt and I walked him back towards the front door.

Gracie sat on the stairs inside the door, coloring with colored pencils.

I stopped placing my hand directly on her left arm, *You want to come eat honey?*

Her feet wiggled to a standing position with a smile on her face. I reached for her hand as we walked towards the kitchen.

My eye contact with Elizabeth confirmed it was time to eat.

Okay, ladies let's do this!

Everyone mingled making their plates and grabbing a drink previously fixed.

Hey, would y'all rather sit on the front porch to eat today?"

Everyone looked at me smiling,

"Yes."
"Yes."
"Oh boy, yes."

Everyone scattered out across the front shaded porch and partially shaded steps. A shy bird sat on the far edge of the porch.

The surrounding trees flowed back and forth, with breezy flutters of the wind across our ears.

Meanwhile, my eyes squint at the watch strapped on my arm. The shorthand was on the one and the longhand was on the twelve. Back in the studio, I stood at the end of the workstation ready for class to begin.

Soon everyone nestled in their seats.

I laid another watercolor sheet on the table in front of each chair. In a structural manner, I covered the bases of watercolor painting.

I encouraged everyone to pick a scene around us at the art studio to paint. As a result, this shuffled our feet.

From afar, I saw a truck pull in the driveway. The closer it got I saw it was Shane.

He stepped out of the truck. Jeans covered his legs. An old navy blue t-shirt covered his upper body. His brown work boots carried him to the top of the porch steps.

I lean under his armpit. Hugging. "Hello everyone." Those who stood in listening distance spoke back.

Then he questioned, "Where are the girls?"

When I peeked my head in the door, both girls stood there. *Daddy's here to take y'all out for dinner. Grab your bags.*

Elizabeth's bag draped long ways across her chest. I watched Gracie dart in the kitchen. She shrugged her shoulders. Then she chuckled.

When she returned I wondered, *What is it, honey?* "Nothing, one lady was playing a joke on me." *Okay, have fun with daddy.*

Class continued after I kissed
Shane, "goodbye".

My hand slipped the on/off radio
switch. Tunes of worship music
pushed across the rooms and the
outdoors of the property as
everyone worked on their painting.

I walked around to each one with
small equal amounts of timing
helping them, coaching them,
instructing them and getting to
know each one better.

Time grew closer to the end of the
afternoon class, meaning dinner
was fast approaching our
scheduled time.

I asked as everyone stood in front
of me, *Who wants to freshen up
and run to town for dinner?*

*Nothing fancy guys. In fact, wear
what is on your body. We will eat
at the local pizza and ice cream
shop.*

Everyone cheered the suggestion.

Good, let's do it. Put your supplies back in the cabinet and place your sheets on the drying table.

Everyone did so and hurried to their rooms to put a sparkling touch to themselves. The sun was dropping behind the trees.

We piled into my car with just enough space.

I drove us to town.

Next to the door, I put the car in park. Everyone climbed out the car.

I tossed my keys in my oversize purse.

We walked in standing in front of the hostess stand.

"How many?"

I look behind me, *seven.*

We followed behind the girl holding menus and utensils wrapped in white napkins in her hands.

Jeni Lynn slid right into the booth first. The rest of us followed. We had plenty of room with space between each of us.

A small table with four chairs sat near our booth.

Harper opened a menu.
A waitress, dressed in a red shirt
with black jeans, walked over to
the end of our booth.

An apron tied loose around her
neck. She grabbed her pen from
the flat pocket sewn near the
navel.

"Drinks anyone?"

From one side of the booth to the
other we, each spoke up with our
drink order at heart.

water
lemonade
sweet tea
dr. pepper
water
diet coke
sweat tea

Each time the waitress wrote the
drinks on her hand.

"I'll be right back ladies."

Soon she returned setting each
drink in front of the correct person.

"Ready to order?"

On her ticket pad she pulled from
the same apron pocket, she wrote
each order promptly.

large pepperoni
medium veggie
medium house
sweet bbq wings
spinach salad

When she left, talk circled the
booth table among us. The art
retreat was the conversation.
Some gradually talked of their
everyday life.

I noticed a lady out of the corner
of my eye. She appeared my age
pushing a heavy lady in a
wheelchair. She pushed her as
close as she could to the small
table next to us. The waitress took
their drink order.

After the waitress sat the two drinks on the table next to us, she walked back to the kitchen where she found our order ready.

Her body frame faced our booth with one pizza in hand and the rest on a big round tray.

When everyone had their food in front of them she asked, "Can I get y'all anything else?"

I looked around the table.

"Does anyone need anything else?" Looking up, *No, we are fine. Thank you.*

She turns to the small table next to us taking their order.

When the waitress finished she left their table walking over to the computer punching in their order.

The lady in the wheelchair asked the lady she was with for her cell phone.

Because her body faced toward our booth most everything, she spoke of traveled nearing our ears. "Yes, I need to make an appointment to see the doctor."

"A rash."

"1:45, tomorrow."

"On my abdomen."

My eyes grew as big as saucers.

The ladies around my table looked
at each other.

The waitress brought our check to
us once we pushed our dishes to
the center of the table.

I placed my credit card downward
for payment.

The waitress ran my credit card.

She returned my card. I wrote Colossians 4:2 with a smiley face next to it at the bottom of the receipt. Then I scribbled in a number for a tip.

We return to the art studio straight up at 7.

Shane text me letting me know the girls and him were home, *they are in bed*.

Class started.

We did our night exercise, a step-by-step watercolor of the lighthouse from Biloxi, Mississippi.

Nine o'clock came fast, and I wrapped class up quick. The slender, white, moon hung in the west. Everyone appeared tired.

Good-bye.

I drove home.

I arrived back at the studio by 8 o'clock the next morning.

Breakfast.

Workspace and nice and neat class started at 9 am sharp.

Today is our last day together.
We will finish up our hand scrap
page by helping it COME ALIVE.

We learned Friday how YOU ARE
ART. Because we are created by
the only one true ARTIST.

We created the foundation of our
art piece using our scraps from
our everyday life.

These scraps represent our life,
the foundation of our life, what
surrounds us, what goes on in our
everyday life.

Then on Saturday recognizing,
those scraps from our everyday
life glued together as texture,
lumps, bumps and shapes of
different sizes appeared.

IN THE MIDDLE of our everyday
life, the foundation of our life is
lumpy and bumpy.

Our traced hands on top of the scraps represent that IN THE MIDDLE of our life it can be messy, lumpy and bumpy, not always smooth.

Today we will use the same art piece, our foundation with our hands IN THE MIDDLE of our lump, bumpy life.

Let's add color, a few designs and so forth to living it up, help it COME ALIVE.

This will represent that no matter what life brings into your life, live ALIVE.

Every day bring your life ALIVE.

COME ALIVE.

I suggest you use the black sharpie again and create fingernails on your traced hands.

Once complete you will paint the fingernails. Use the different colored sharpies.

Other ways to add color add:
a bracelet
a sun
clouds
house
flowers
doodle
words
laundry basket
airplane
birds
dog
food
a cross
music notes

Anything representing your daily life place on the hands or background area.

My eyes wandered across the table watching each one add color to their masterpiece.

Eleven o'clock fast approached.

A helicopter flew over shaking everything in the studio. Outside, I saw the shadow of the copter and a yellow butterfly flew by as the trees swayed back and forth in the wind.

I instructed everyone in using a sheet of paper from the stack at the end of the table.

Please write what this experience has been for you. Share ways I can pray for you. I will treasure your words and pray over any matter.

The class was over at that moment.

We ate lunch.

Then everyone headed upstairs gathering their belongings and finish packing.

By 2 o'clock, everyone was gone from the studio.

Shane, Elizabeth, Gracie and I cheered giving each other high fives and half hugs.

We did it!

Monday came sudden.

I dropped Gracie off at school. As a local, I knew Target does not open until 8 am.

I sat still in my car.

A car pulled into a parking place near the front door. A lady dressed in a dark color business suit got out.

In a fast motion, her feet appeared in front of the stores double sliding glass doors.

A sudden tilt forward, she plopped back on her heals. A slight lean to her right, she turned facing her car.

Another fast motion of walking she hopped back in her car, driving away.

The clock on the upper right-hand side of my GPS read 7:24 am.

My back faced the sun.

My front faced a police car that pulled into the parking lot at the same time as me.

We parked 3 rows across from one another.

My left hand reached pulling my sun visor. The light on my mirror came on as I opened it.

Below the visor, slight to the left, out the corner of my eye, I could see the police car parked. Its taillights faced me.

Since it was a police car and one of the few cars in the parking lot my eyes continued gravitating nearby watching it.

Moments later a black four-door jeep pulled perfectly into the parking space next to the police car. I put on a "people watching" hat.

The jeep faced my direction. I saw the driver of the jeep was a male.

My thoughts ponder on, *oh it's a buddy dropping something off to one of his friends.*

The police car door flung open.

A black tactical boot hit the pavement. The body moved away from the car. I could see the body figure was of a female.

The jeeps' driver door flung open.

Before the driver got out, the police wedged herself in the doorway. She fell in his arms landing a big long kiss on his lips.

Never mind people speeding, houses broke in, others in need or breaking the law.

I grabbed my makeup bag from
my backseat.

I applied:

original foundation primer
long wear concealer
studio fix powder
perfect flush blush
urban decay eye shadow
large lash mascara
lip balm

Once my makeup was complete, I pushed my visor.

My mirror smashed closed.

The police car drove away.

The jeep driver wearing a red worker shirt walked inside Target.

At 8 o'clock, I entered the store.

My day was full of errands.

At the end of it though, the carpool line never looked so good.

I thought of the art retreat. So grateful for the many blessings God provided.

I am not just lucky.

I am blessed.

My mind pondered over the two, lucky and blessed. After realizing there is a BIG divergence between the two, my eyes glanced in my passenger side mirror where they remained glued for the next several minutes.

A stretcher rolled to the back of the ambulance.

I saw the whole thing.

The football players were exiting the gym's back door crossing the school street to the field.

As the players remain crossing, I noticed one running out the gym sided door. He lingered through the carpool line.

First in front of the car next to me, he crossed. Then crossing in front of me.

Instantly, I glanced in my mirror.

My first response was to lay on
my horn.

I did just that.

A roaring burst of horn flowed loud
far and wide.

My voice did too!

S
T
O
P
!

Usually, my windows are rolled downward while I sit in the carpool line. This early in August the temperature leaves my face bright red. So, I kept my windows rolled up with my air conditioner functioning wide open.

My scream was so loud my ears hurt. I wondered how no one heard me.

It took place so fast!

My eyeballs saw everything.

Today was the first day of school. I did not want to witness this.

Everything was a domino effect, sight, sound, sight, sound, sight, sound.

It hurt me to SEE!

The moment my hand touched the horn was the moment a fourth of a second earlier I saw a car coming. Boy and car touch!

My cell phone fumbled in my hands. I called 911. Unclear how many people saw. How many called. My car door opened, I walked over one step away from the boy.

I share this with you so calm. Who am I kidding, I did not walk. I raced extremely fast no one was able to see me.

My knees rested on the hot blackish pavement. I reached for his teen resembling wrist.

There was a pulse.

"Thank you, Jesus!"

A crowd gathered.

When the ambulance arrived, I drifted back to my car.

Tears streamed my cheeks.

Elizabeth ambled over to her car parked along the fence. She put her book bag in her trunk.

I saw her looking.

Soon she appeared at my car window. She could tell I had been crying. "Mom, are you okay?"

"I am honey!"

"I saw everything."

After my heart spilled the entire story in Elizabeth's ears, she stepped near the edge of the crowd. I noticed her talking to her friends. My head laid back resting on my seat.

Elizabeth dashed toward my car. She blurts out while knocking on my window, "It's him, mom."

"It's Noah!"

Author's Note

Dream for a second, this story line, *Under Contract*, is based off a real life dream of mine (owning my own art studio). After much prayer and walking in obedience, the Lord directed my path writing a story about it instead. As usual, He works His best in unexpected ways.

   After the writing of my first book, *Daddy's Briefcase: My Journey through Liver Cancer*, I claimed not to write another one. Not long after, I felt the Holy Spirit prompt me in writing again. Unsure what exactly this meant, I listened for His still quiet voice. First thought, a follow up of my first book. Then, I walked through an unexplained time of darkness. My world was upside down. My entire family was puzzled. No one knew what happen to me. Yet alone, nor did I. I have been through some hard times in my life. Certain this topped it, while at its current state. On the other side of it, I knew He wanted me to write again. Still not sure, I aimed towards the follow up book. The anxiety every time I sat to write was overwhelming. In those moments, He redirected me to fiction. He whispered, "go have fun". And that I did. The process of *Under Contract* started. Through His mercy and grace, I over came the dark while writing this book during a period of three-years. When He said, "speed up". I did. When He said, "slow down". I did. That my friend is the joy of serving an awesome God.

I hope this provides encouragement to all. No matter where you are or what season of life you are in, do what you are wired to do. Find a way to do it where you are. You are awesome. You are loved. You are art. Let your light SHINE. Matthew 5:16

Dream,
Ashley Murphy

Acknowledgements

Writing a book is like birthing a child. Only, it takes longer then nine months. In addition, it truly takes a community to help with the birthing.

I am very thankful for my family: Husband, thanks for continuing to believe in me. Your countless words of "we could make millions" are priceless. Clearly, I know my writing is more than money. As we collaborate to navigate this thing called parenting in this season of our life, I am thankful it is fitting I work from home.

Child, Katelyn, thanks for your endless time in guiding me through out the process of writing this book. Your expertise in writing helped tremulously navigate the editing process. So glad you were for hire. Most people do not get the privilege of their daughter working for them. Especially editing their book, I will gladly write a letter of recommendation anytime.

Child, Karly, you probably heard more than anyone, "Wait just a sec while I do this for my book." or "No, I can't right now. I've got to do this for my book." You also always gave great advise on the book along the way. Thank you for your helpful and understanding heart. You are my little sidekick for life.

Beyond my family, each one who walked alongside of me when I talked about "my book" this or that:
Compel Family
Dream Catchers Group
Pen Pal
Fibrolamellar Family
Blog Readers
My writer friends.
My new writer friend, Courtney, whom the Lord graciously placed in my life at MOMs. Her perspective words when I asked for prayers during the editing process, "At least you have something to edit."

Bible study friends, each one of you, even though you claim not to read, you will one day in your next season of life. Each of you mean more to my soul than you will ever know. I am thankful He has crossed our paths. May the Lord continue to bless you.

Those who asked about my book along the way.

Those who encouraged me, my soul is fueled off encouragement.

Those who I had to say "no" to.

You, my reader, for taking the time to embark this journey with me. It brings great joy to share this verse novel with you personally. Please share with a friend, post a picture of your copy of *Under Contract* on your social media and/or write a review somewhere, such as Amazon.

Last, but not least, my Savior, Jesus Christ. Thank you, thank you for filling me up to run over into the world, your kingdom. I love being yours.

www.ingramcontent.com/pod-product-compliance
Lightning Source LLC
Chambersburg PA
CBHW060324260626
47160CB00007B/2674